Ask your bookseller for books you have missed or visit us at cyoa.com to collect them all.

CURSE OF THE PIRATE MIST

BY DOUG WILHELM

ILLUSTRATED BY VLADIMIR SEMIONOV
COVER ILLUSTRATED BY GABHOR UTOMO

CHOOSECO®
WAITSFIELD, VERMONT

Illustrated by: Vladimir Semionov
Cover Art: Gabhor Utomo
Book Design: Julia Gignoux, Freedom Hill Design and Book Production

For information regarding permission, write to:

CHOOSECO®
P.O. Box 46
Waitsfield, Vermont 05673
www.cyoa.com

ISBN-13: 978-1-937133-02-3
ISBN-10: 1-937133-02-8

Published simultaneously in the United States and Canada

Printed in the Canada

0 9 8 7 6 5 4 3 2 1

*This book is dedicated to
Ray Montgomery*

BEWARE and WARNING!

This book is different from other books.

You and YOU ALONE are in charge of what happens in this story.

There are dangers, choices, adventures, and consequences. YOU must use all of your numerous talents and much of your enormous intelligence. The wrong decision could end in disaster—even death. But, don't despair. At any time, YOU can go back and make another choice, alter the path of your story, and change its result.

Your uncle writes best-selling books about high-stakes adventure. He lives life like the heroes of his novels—fast-paced and exciting! Since your parents are stationed overseas, you are his travel buddy. His latest research leads you both to Guyana, in hopes of chasing down a sunken ship rumored to contain a treasure worth three TRILLION dollars. The sunken treasure has captured the interest of lots of different people, the rich and powerful among them. You're intrigued by tales of a strange purple mist that overtakes those who get too close to the treasure. Will you and your uncle find fame, glory, or the plot of his next novel?

Or will you wind up as shark bait?!

"Are you doing anything important right now?" your uncle asks.

"Not really," you say without looking up from your laptop.

"Good. You need to pack."

Now you look up. Your uncle has an excited gleam in his eye.

You ask, "Why do I need to pack?"

He doesn't answer right away. Your uncle's a writer, he loves to build suspense.

Instead of answering, your uncle walks through his cluttered apartment, pausing in front of an old-time deep-sea diver's outfit. Made of heavy canvas and thick metal weights, the thing stands in the corner like some weird suit of armor, topped by its huge copper helmet with the thick glass portholes.

Walking past the suit, your uncle pauses by a shelf that displays some broken pottery from an ancient Greek ship that sank in the Mediterranean Sea. There's also a small mound of antique Spanish coins, crude but valuable, recovered from a wreck in the Caribbean Sea. And there's your favorite relic from his adventures: a flintlock pistol, of polished wood and brass, that your uncle swears was wielded by a real-life pirate, some 300 years ago.

Passing by those treasures, he picks up a globe. He walks toward you, pointing at it.

You lean close, peering.

You say, "We're going to *Guyana*?"

Turn to the next page.

Grinning, your uncle nods. "Yep! Did you know it's the only English-speaking country in South America?"

"Um...I've never actually, technically, heard of it before," you say.

His face lights up. "Never heard of *Guyana*?" He pronounces it *Guy-AH-na*. "Guyana's on the southern edge of the Caribbean region," he says. "Right on the old pirate coast."

Now you're beginning to get it.

"Has somebody found something? Is that why we're going?"

"Not just *something*," your uncle says. "This could be the biggest find of all. Pack fast! Our plane leaves in three hours."

Flying south from Miami on Caribbean Airlines, all you see below is blue, blue water.

"It's a very *interesting* situation," your uncle says. He writes books about big-money, high-stakes treasure hunts. You've been living with him while your parents are stationed overseas, and you've learned that, to your uncle, *interesting* can mean a lot of things. *Exciting. Mysterious. Dangerous.*

Turn to page 4.

4

It also can mean: someone has a chance to get rich. Very rich. And it could be him.

"If you've read my books, and I'm *sure* you have," he says with a sly smile, "then you know there's huge interest in finding what are often called treasure ships. These can go back to the 1500s and 1600s, when Spain was the first to colonize Central and South America. The Spaniards were obsessed with gold and silver. They extracted it in vast amounts, and then shipped it home in tall, fat sailing vessels.

"It wasn't long before the first Caribbean pirates began attacking those ships," he tells you. "Sometimes they got the gold—but sometimes they sent the ship to the bottom. With the treasure inside."

"Okay. So somebody's found a Spanish treasure ship?"

Go on to the next page.

"Nope! But that's how the legends of pirates and treasure got started. With today's underwater-search technology, salvagers sometimes find wrecks with holds full of gold bars, silver coins—you name it. These discoveries can be worth millions. So when someone says they've found a treasure ship...well, the world pays attention."

"I'm paying attention," you say.

"I see that. So here's what happened..."

Later, as your plane approaches Guyana's capital, you ponder what you've heard.

"So," you say, "nobody's ever heard of these guys who claim they found the shipwreck?"

"Nope—it's like they came out of nowhere," your uncle says. "Catchy name, though. Treasurizers, Inc."

"And they say a British freighter got torpedoed off Guyana in World War II."

"Yes, and that's believable," he says. "Back then, Guyana was a British colony and a key source of bauxite, a mineral used to make aluminum for airplanes and lots else. Bauxite was vital to the war effort—so German U-boats prowled these waters, hunting for freighters carrying the mineral to England. They sank dozens."

"But," you say, "*this* ship was different."

Turn to page 7.

"Right. It had a super-secret mission. See, in those dark early days of the war, Germany had conquered all of Europe, and Hitler was preparing to invade England. Treasurizers says the Brits decided to ship out their core wealth—all the gold, silver, and jewels the government had locked away. Nobody wanted the Nazis to get *that*."

"So," you say, "the British loaded an ordinary freighter with the richest cargo ever. And right before the ship reached their South American colony, a U-boat sank it."

"That's what Treasurizers claims. They say they've found the wreck, and they want investors to bankroll the salvage operation. The payoff could be fantastic."

"It's almost too good to be true," you say.

Your uncle smiles. "Welcome to the crazy world of treasure hunting."

As you step out of the plane, the tropical heat hits you like surging steam. Walking down the metal stairs, you gaze around at a flat, green landscape. It's sunny, very humid, and really hot.

You walk toward a low, clean-looking white building that's the main terminal at Cheddi Jagan International Airport. Inside it's shady, and cooler. It seems to take forever to get through customs, where your passport is finally stamped by a relaxed official in a short-sleeved uniform.

Turn to the next page.

Now your uncle is striding toward the exit, pulling his wheeled suitcase behind.

"Let's grab a taxi!" he calls back to you.

Through the open doors ahead, bright sunlight shimmers. But as you start to follow, an olive-skinned man in a dark suit hurries up to your uncle.

"Sir," the man announces. "I am here to drive you."

"What? Oh, I'm sorry," your uncle says. "I think you've mistaken us for someone else."

"No," the man says firmly. "You are Benjamin Starkwell, the author, yes? Here for the treasure ship."

"Yes, that's me. But how...?"

"I have orders from Treasurizers to drive you to your hotel!" the man declares.

"But I didn't arrange for a ride," your uncle says. "How did you even know...?"

"Just come," the man says, and he reaches for the suitcase. "I will take this."

Something about this doesn't seem quite right.

As you watch, another voice beside you whispers: "Treasure ship?"

You turn to see a boy. About your age, he's darker skinned than the man talking with your uncle. He wears shorts, flip-flops, and a white T-shirt with the image of a flag—a red triangle on a yellow triangle, on a green background.

Turn to page 10.

"You come 'bout the treasure ship," he whispers in a soft, gentle accent. "I know something 'bout that."

"You do?"

He nods. "Come with me. I will take you to someone."

"Okay, we're all set!" your uncle says. "This man works for Treasurizers. I'm not sure how they knew we were coming, but he'll take us in a limousine to the Princess Hotel. You'll love it there—nicest hotel in Guyana. Air-conditioning, pool…"

You step closer, and whisper to him about the boy. Your uncle glances at him skeptically.

"Look," he says to you, "It's not safe to go off with people we don't know."

"But," you say, "how did that driver guy know we were coming? What if it's *him* who's not safe?"

Your uncle shrugs. "I'm sure he's fine. Well, hey—either way, our adventure starts here. You decide our first move. Which should it be?"

If you go with the driver sent by Treasurizers, go on to the next page.

If you go with the boy who says he knows something, turn to page 71.

Outside the terminal, you stop.

"This is a *limo*?"

The man in the suit has led you to a plain white sedan. He's got the trunk open and is loading in your luggage.

Your uncle shrugs. "Guyana's a very poor country," he explains. "A lot of what's ordinary back home is luxury here. Nice car!" he tells the man.

"Thank you." The man opens the back door.

Turn to the next page.

The road into Georgetown, Guyana's capital, is edged with sand and low-lying white buildings. The cars and trucks are small and mostly battered. You are surrounded by evidence of Guyana's poverty.

But when you pull up at the Princess Hotel, you yelp, "Whoa!" Georgetown's glitziest hotel spreads out wide, tall, and gleaming.

Inside, the lobby has shining floors, white-leather furniture, and lots more glass. Perched on a long white couch is a woman with spiky short hair. She looks up from an expensive-looking laptop and spots you and your uncle.

"Why, it's Benjamin Starkwell, best-seller!"

"Hey there, Lacey. So you're involved in this business?"

"Are you kidding?" She glances dramatically around. "*Everybody*'s interested in this business, Ben. Who's your young friend?"

Your uncle introduces you. "Lacey's a treasure …enthusiast," he tells you.

"Oh, tell the kid the truth. I'm a crazy lady with far too much money, and too much time for getting into trouble."

She glances around again. "Ben, we *have* to talk. Immediately. *Privately.*"

"Lacey, we just got here," your uncle says. "We have to check in."

"Then do! But both of you," she says, "come to my suite in ten minutes. You *won't* be sorry."

Turn to page 14.

As your uncle fills out paperwork at the long check-in counter, an elevator door opens. A sharply dressed man steps out and strides your way, trailed by two beefy guys wearing sunglasses.

The smooth man walks up to your uncle. He doesn't glance your way, but one of the shades-wearers—they're clearly security men—gives you a stern looking over, like he's inspecting you for weapons. You feel a chill.

Go on to the next page.

"Ben Starkwell? Well, of course it is," says the first man. He's very self-assured. But your uncle, turning from the counter, doesn't seem to know him.

"Hello," your uncle says, puzzled yet polite.

"I'm Jeremy Girond," the man says, extending his hand. "CEO of Treasurizers."

"Ah! Well, it's great to meet you," says your uncle, interested now. He introduces you, but the man, dressed with tropical elegance in a silken gray shirt and ivory-white slacks, barely glances your way.

"I'm so glad that Jagad, my driver, found you at the airport," Girond says. "I wanted to make sure you got here safely. There are a lot of sharks around here, you know."

He smiles, showing very white teeth.

Yeah—a lot of sharks, your intuition seems to whisper in your ear. *And you're one of them.*

Though he's polite, your uncle still seems puzzled.

"We appreciated the ride, Mr. Girond," he says, "but how on earth did you know we were arriving just then? I'm sure we've never met, or been in touch."

Turn to the next page.

Girond's smile is wide, yet a little chilly. "It's my business to know who's interested in our project, Mr. Starkwell."

That's not really an explanation, you think.

You don't like this guy, but you can tell your uncle is intrigued. He's got a nose for a good story. And, you realize, powerful people who don't want to explain themselves can make for great stories.

If you can find the truth.

Girond looks around the lobby like he's about to share a secret. He leans toward your uncle. When you take a step, to hear better, the security man glares. But you're still close enough to hear.

"I want to give you the inside story—an exclusive," Girond murmurs in your uncle's ear. "The location of our find is, of course, a *closely* guarded secret. But tomorrow morning at eleven, we're taking a small group of potential...supporters out to the site. We want them—and you—to glimpse what we've found.

"You'll get a look through our cameras. You'll be the first people outside Treasurizers to see the wreck itself. Your book will just about write itself!

"We'll expect you at eleven," Girond says.

It isn't a question. Girond seems to be informing your uncle that things will go a certain way.

His way.

Go on to the next page.

A few minutes later, having dumped your luggage in your small hotel room, you two are sitting in the luxurious suite of Lacey Hastings.

"I tell you, Ben, this is a *weird* one," she says to your uncle.

"There's always weirdness when big money's involved," your uncle says.

"And big money is *way* involved here," Lacey says. She grins. "For example, I'm here!"

You like Lacey. She's full of life. Her smile is joyful and sincere, unlike Jeremy Girond's.

"Anyway, get this," she tells you both. "The buzz here is that when some local fishermen accidentally got too close to the secret shipwreck site, they were engulfed by a weird purple fog. They couldn't see a thing. They were lost at sea for twenty-four hours!"

Your uncle gives a skeptical grimace. "Come on," he says. "Purple fog?"

"I know! It could be just a silly rumor—pure folklore," Lacey says. "Or it *might* be a clever way to protect the site. You know, spread this rumor that scares people away from snooping around out there. They don't want anyone scooping their big treasure hunt."

"Treasure hunters are deadly serious about security," your uncle tells you.

"But guess what? Ben, I've *found* it," Lacey says. "I've located their site."

Turn to the next page.

Your uncle's eyes go wide. "Seriously?"

"Yes! And I want to take you there. Tomorrow morning. Ben, the star of your book is going to be *me*."

"Lacey," your uncle says, "if Treasurizers wants to keep their site a big secret, how did *you* find out?"

"Well," she answers, smiling, "let's just say that in the age of Google Earth, when ordinary people can gain access to satellite images, it's possible to monitor an area like the coastal waters of Guyana. If you see a lot of activity within a certain set of coordinates, you can find those coordinates. You can locate that activity.

"Then," she says, "using side-scan sonar imaging equipment, you can take your yacht out to that location—okay, it helps if you're an ordinary person with a whole lot of money. And you can *find* the location of that wreck."

"So," your uncle says, "you've been out there? On your boat?"

Go on to the next page.

"Not *yet*," she says. "This is where you have such great timing. We're going out tomorrow morning—at nine sharp. Ben, these Treasurizer guys are trying to raise big money, so they can mount a first-class salvage operation. They've invited wealthy investors down, to see. They invited me!

"But, you see," Lacey says with a smile that's now sly, "I don't have to wait. I can hit that wreck *fast*. Tomorrow, we take a run out there. Get a bunch of readings, build a digital image of the site. Get back before anyone knows we were there. See how real this thing actually is.

"Purple mist," she snorts. "*Pfah!*"

Turn to page 21.

As the sun sets in Guyana, you sit beside the hotel pool. Fiery red streaks run along the deepening blue sky, with thin clouds like trails of smoke up there. This is the first tropical sunset of your life— and you'll always remember it.

"We've got a choice to make," your uncle declares.

"I can tell you want to go with Treasurizers," you say.

"Well, those guys *are* the main players here," he says. "They found the wreck, they're bringing in the investors, they've got the salvage vessel. Lacey's got a yacht. She may be able to learn something about the site, *if* she's really found it. But Treasurizers has already claimed this shipwreck. They're not going to want some rich lady sweeping in with her sonar."

"You mean Lacey could be in danger?"

"Maybe," he says. "If she's smart, she'll zoom out and back before anyone notices—but she is taking a risk."

"But I feel like she's a nice person," you say. "That Girond guy—I don't trust him."

"Well, going out with Lacey *would* be an adventure," your uncle admits. "We could get an unsupervised look at the site. But I don't want to anger Treasurizers. They're the main players here.

"Time to decide," he says. "Do we take our first trip with crazy Lacey—or slick Girond? Either way works for me. What about you?"

If you go with Lacey, turn to the next page.

If you go with Treasurizers, turn to page 38.

"I want to go out with Lacey first," you say. "I bet Treasurizers will never know. Plus, they need you. Girond wants you to make him famous—just like Lacey does."

"True," your uncle says. "Okay, I'll put Treasurizers off for a day. But I do have one issue about going out there with Lacey." He trails one toe in the water.

"What is it?"

"Well...I'd really rather you didn't come."

"*What*?"

"Look, I won't lie—Lacey's plan is risky. You saw those security guys in the lobby. Sailing out to poke around the site of the shipwreck—even just at the surface—could be dangerous."

Go on to the next page.

"I'd like to leave you here as my base camp," he says. "We'll stay connected by radio phone. That way, if anything goes wrong, you can send out help. I'll give you an emergency contact number, just in case."

"No way! I want to go."

"I understand, and I can't force you to stay—but I'm *asking* you," he says. "It's important for us to work as a team, and what I'd like you to do is pretty important. Be my base camp and emergency dispatcher."

You ponder this as night falls. Suddenly, a million stars are reflected in the still, dark water of the hotel pool.

If you decide to go, turn to the next page.

If you decide to stay, turn to page 27.

The next morning you're out on *Lace Curtain*, Lacey's gleaming white yacht. Crew members bring you sodas and snacks as the cabin cruiser zips across the water. About an hour out from shore, the coastal water turns from muddy brown to deep blue-green.

Above you, Lacey looks down from the flying bridge and announces, "This is the spot!"

Nobody on the yacht notices a thin black rod, like a probe, that emerges from the water nearby. The slight hissing sound it produces is softer than the gentle slapping of the ocean water against the side of the *Lace Curtain*.

Turn to page 26.

There's a shout from up above. You both look up to see Lacey lurch away from the controls on the flying bridge.

"Ben! Starboard!"

On the right side of the yacht, a dense purple mist seems to be billowing up from the water itself. You can't see a thing through it—nor, at this point, can Ben, Lacey, or the crew.

None of you spots the mini-submarine as it surfaces around the nozzle that's issuing the fog.

The purple mist fascinates you. So that rumor was true! But *why*?

Peering into the mist, you have a moment's fantasy that the ghost of an old-time Caribbean pirate, maybe Blackbeard with a brace of pistols and candles burning in his beard, will clamber aboard your boat.

Then you do see a dark figure. It slips on board from the deck of the sub. Another one follows.

But these aren't ghosts. In the fog that turns people into shapes, you can see they've got guns. And now they're pointing them.

There's a ripping sound, and Lacey falls from the bridge. She hits the water with a splash. Horrified, you turn away as the mist swallows you up on the rear deck.

You don't hear the second burst of gunfire. That's the one aimed at your uncle. And at you.

The End

You're on the radio phone in your hotel room. Your uncle, at the other end, is excited—Lacey has just announced they've found the spot.

Then you hear sounds of confusion.

Your uncle's voice crackles: "Hey, what..."

In the background you hear Lacey: "Ben, do you see that?"

He says, "Yeah! Lacey, watch out—it's coming up fast!"

Alarmed, you shout into the phone, "What? What's coming up?"

Your uncle says, "I don't know. It's purple, it's like a fog. I can't see the bridge! Lacey, can you see anything from there? I can't..."

You hear a ripping sound, like gunfire. You hear a scream: "Help! They're shooting!"

Your uncle shouts, "Lacey! Hey no, don't..."

There's another burst of gunfire, then a loud thud. And the phone goes dead.

"Hello?" You shout, "Ben. Ben! Pick up, okay? Ben!"

But there is no answer. Somehow you know there won't be an answer.

You're in a hotel room in Guyana.

And now you're all alone.

Desperately, you keep trying to reach your uncle on the radiophone, but there's no answer. You know in your gut that something is very wrong.

Turn to the next page.

You call the emergency number your uncle gave you. It reaches the national police, but no one there seems at all interested. You can tell they know you're a kid, and an American.

Your uncle left you with his traveler's checks, plus some local money. You take out a Guyanese $20 bill and look at it. On the back is a picture of a big steel ship. You wonder, *Is my uncle lying on the bottom of the ocean, by the wreck of that treasure-smuggling freighter?*

You take a deep breath. You open the door, and walk to the elevator.

You feel relieved when you leave the hotel. Something about that fancy place just felt *wrong*. Out in front of the hotel, a white sedan like the taxi from the airport pulls up to the curb.

You don't even have time to react as the passenger's front door is flung open, and a man leaps out and grabs you by the arms.

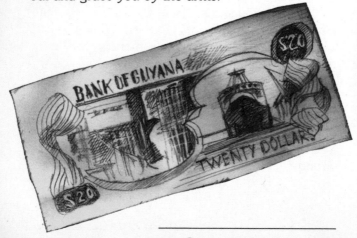

Go on to the next page.

As you're shoved forward, a door is popped open from inside the car. You're shoved through it onto the back seat.

The front passenger door pops open. You hear the man fling himself in. When the car shoots ahead, with a shriek of tires, you roll back hard against the seat. Terrified, you struggle to sit up.

It's no use yelling or screaming. You've got your cell phone in your pocket, but there's nobody to call. Instead you sit watchful and silent as the car threads its way, too fast, through clusters of traffic that come up suddenly, then are disappearing behind you.

The man who grabbed you whirls around—with both hands he seizes your head, and shoves you down hard. He pushes you down even farther, until you're jammed onto the floor between the seats.

Your head and neck twist painfully as he gives you one last hard shove.

"You *stay* down," he says.

Turn to the next page.

When the car finally lurches to a stop, the man in the passenger seat looks down at you. You're surprised when he speaks in a calming, soft, Guyanese-accented voice.

"Okay, you can sit up now," he says. "We goin' to go inside together. Very cool and normal, okay? That way you don' get hurt. Okay?"

Swallowing hard, you nod. He reaches down, takes your hand, and helps you up.

Now you're walking between the two men, into the featureless white block of a downtown building.

Upstairs is a small apartment that's almost bare. Through a single window, you see a sign atop a building across the street—*Salt & Pepper Food Court*. Then the man who was driving yanks down a shade.

The room is almost dark. Neither guy turns on a light. Instead, they question you.

"Where you staying?"

"Why are you walking alone?"

"Who you here with? How much will they pay to get you back?"

These guys, you realize, have nothing to do with the treasure hunt. They saw you walking alone with a backpack, looking like a tourist's kid, and they grabbed you.

They're after money, plain and simple.

On impulse, you decide to tell them the truth.

Go on to the next page.

You tell the kidnappers about Treasurizers, Inc., and the shipwreck with secret riches that they claim to have found. You tell them about the murder of your uncle, and the threat against you.

"This man in charge—the rich one," the driver says. "Would you know him? If you saw him again?"

"Well, sure." You remember Jeremy Girond's elegant tropical clothes. "Yeah."

The kidnappers nod at each other.

"Let's go," they say to you.

A few minutes later you're back outside the Princess Hotel.

At least two hours drag by. You're thinking of just handing the kidnappers your money and traveler's checks, then bolting from the car. But where would you go? What would you do?

You're wracking your brain for a better idea when Jeremy Girond emerges from the hotel entrance, and climbs into a waiting silver SUV.

You say, "That's him! In the SUV."

The driver nods, waits for the vehicle to turn onto the street, then pulls out to follow.

You wonder what these guys think they're going to accomplish, following the wealthy head of a treasure-salvage company through the streets of Georgetown.

But it turns out they know exactly what they're doing.

Turn to the next page.

With surprisingly nimble skills, your driver tails the silver SUV, staying just far enough behind not to be spotted. The pursuit takes you into an area of boxy, featureless buildings of decaying wood and corrugated metal. As you turn a corner, you see a flash of water ahead.

You're in a neighborhood of storage buildings, probably by the harbor.

On a cramped street, the SUV stops in front of a windowless metal building. It looks like a big long storage unit. It's got a tan metal door with a big padlock. Your car stops, a block away.

Jeremy Girond steps out of the SUV. So does a man in a dark suit. It's the oddly sinister driver who brought you from the airport.

As Girond watches, the driver opens the padlock with a key. They go inside the storage building, closing its door behind them.

The driver of your car turns to you.

"Go over there," he says. "Throw open that door."

"*What?*"

Go on to the next page.

He nods. "Tell them you know what they're doing. Say it loud: *I know what you're doing!* Then run."

"Why would I do *that*?"

"Because if you don't do that, we'll kill you. Right here," the driver says in his soft accent.

You walk up to the warehouse door. Half a block behind, the sedan creeps along.

Reaching for the door handle, you pause. Time stands still.

And then you run.

You're expecting to hear gunshots, squealing tires, or both—but there's only the sound of your sneakers on the pavement.

You dash along a maze of featureless streets. Which way should you go? You don't even know where you're going, so you just...keep running.

Then it hits you.

The U.S. Embassy.

You read a novel once about an American who was wrongly accused of espionage in a foreign capital. The secret police were on their way to arrest the hero when a phone call tipped him off. He caught a taxi and outraced his pursuers to the gates of the U.S. Embassy.

An embassy is there to help its country's citizens—to protect them, if necessary. Once he got inside, the hero was safe.

To get to the embassy, you probably just need a taxi. And you've got money. But this is a warehouse district. And you're exhausted.

Turn to the next page.

34

Emerging from a tiny side street, you stumble—unexpectedly—into the middle of a busy road.

It's busy with vehicles and people, and lined with little shops. They've got little awnings outside, as shields from the blazing sun.

A car honks. Leaping out of the way, you fall hard onto the pavement. Another car brakes loudly, swerving around you. You scramble out of the traffic.

People are standing around outside, but nobody seems to have noticed you. Would the kidnappers chase you? Probably not; but after all that's happened, you can't be sure.

The sun is intense. You feel dizzy. You're terribly thirsty. Inside a tiny store, you see colorful soda bottles inside a tall, glass-front cooler. You hurry in, gasping, "Cola? Please?"

A woman, her head wrapped in a colorful scarf, looks up from a counter that's no more than a foot wide.

"Why, honey," she says, "you are all out of breath!"

She hands you a soda and, gratefully, you drink it down.

"Ma'am," you say, "I need a taxi."

The woman leans over her counter, toward the sunshine. In a booming voice, she shouts: "Hey *taxi!*"

No more than five seconds later, a yellow car pulls up. You thank the woman and pull out a Guyanese bill to pay for your soda. But she shakes her head.

"You just get home safe." She says it with a smile that you'll remember forever.

Turn to page 36.

In the sunshine outside the U.S. Embassy, you show your passport and try to explain your plight to a uniformed U.S. Marine who is guarding the gate. He listens, then makes a phone call. In a couple of minutes, a smartly dressed woman strides out from the front door.

"Hello," she says kindly, shaking your sweaty hand. "I'm Regina Smart. Had some trouble?"

You take a breath, hardly knowing where to start. But she holds up one palm.

"Let's go inside, shall we?"

You step with Regina through the doors into the blessedly welcome cool of air-conditioning. Past a very American-looking reception area, the embassy officer brings you through heavy metal security doors, into a hallway lined with little offices. Hers is decorated with potted plants and family photos, and a large wall clock above you. Regina spends a few moments processing your passport, and you stare up at the clock nervously. These moments could be critical to saving your uncle's life!

Finally she turns to you.

Go on to the next page.

"I've located you in the system. Sorry to keep you waiting. Please, tell me what's going on."

Regina's eyes widen but she stays quiet, listening, as you unfold your incredible tale.

When you're finally finished, she says, "And you say your parents are stationed overseas?"

"Yes ma'am," you say.

"Where's their home base?"

You tell her. She nods.

"Looks like I've got some phone calls to make," Regina tells you. She takes a breath. "Your uncle is our next priority," she tells you. "But you are our first. You're safe now, and you're going home. Your adventures are over."

The End

38

You decide to go with the Treasurizers. They take you in a small convoy of cars down to the docks where you board their boat.

Painted blue below the deck and bright white above, the Treasurizers salvage vessel is modern and clean looking, with a squarish structure amidships that is topped by a cluster of impressive antennas.

Girond ushers you two on board. Your uncle gazes all around, clearly hoping for a tour of the deck—but now Girond hurries you inside.

"If you would follow me, please," he says, as he starts you down a narrow metal staircase.

That's the last you'll see of daylight during your voyage on his ship, *Nemo's Dream*.

Go on to the next page.

Below decks, Girond leads to you a chamber that has no windows, no portholes. Instead, one wall is lined with large, flat-screen monitors. You're introduced to two men, sitting before the monitors at keyboards and other controls. Both are wearing blue polo shirts with the Treasurizers logo on their chests.

"These are Gary and Declan," Girond says. "They're our ROV operators."

You whisper to your uncle, "What's an ROV?"

Girond hears you, and smiles. "Sorry for the jargon," he says smoothly—"that means remote-operated vehicle. Today these gentlemen are in charge of providing us with underwater eyes and ears. I know you'll be *very* impressed with what they're going to show."

Girond seems a lot nicer, today. But it's clear that it's he, not the guys in blue shirts, who is in charge.

"I hope you don't mind," he says. "We'll be filming this little expedition today."

"You mean filming underwater?" your uncle asks.

Turn to the next page.

"That too," says Girond. "We'll also film our interactions in here."

He motions to the back wall. You turn to see a young woman, with a blonde ponytail and a Treasurizers shirt, who has a digital video camera trained on you.

Girond's cell phone buzzes. He glances at it.

"If you'll excuse me," he says to your uncle, "our other guests have arrived."

Before slipping out, he smiles charmingly at the camera.

An hour later, you're steaming ahead, somewhere off the coast of Guyana. At least that's what the Treasurizers people say. None of the five guests in this room is permitted to go upstairs to see for themselves.

The others who've joined you in the ROV control room include a handsome, silver-haired gentleman of about 60, an eager young assistant to the silver-maned man—they're both dressed casually, in open-necked shirts—and a very serious woman who seems like a business executive. She's wearing an executive-style pants suit.

The woman keeps pulling out her digital tablet and tapping notes. Your uncle jots notes the old-fashioned way, with a pen and a spiral notebook. The silver-haired gentleman and his assistant watch everything very closely, but say little.

Turn to page 42.

For more than an hour, there is little to see. The monitors are turned off, and the ROV operators just wait. Then, the rolling motion eases and the ship's engine drops to a low purr. As if on cue, Girond appears at the door.

"We're over the site now," he says, and smiles.

"The ROV is being lowered into the water," Girond says. "In just a few minutes, we'll all begin to see what we came here to see."

Again he smiles, like the host of a TV show. But your instincts tell you this guy isn't everything he seems.

"Let me tell you a story," Girond begins.

Go on to the next page.

"In those desperately dark days of 1940, when Germany had conquered all of mainland Europe and the U.S. had yet to enter the war, Great Britain found itself fighting alone," Girond says.

"We all know how perilous Britain's situation seemed at the time, with the Nazi war machine massed just across the English Channel," Girond goes on. "England is a small island, really—and her army was decimated. How could she stop the invasion that everyone believed was coming?

"Prime Minister Winston Churchill was both a patriot and a realist," Girond continues. "With his famous speeches, he rallied the British people—but secretly, he also prepared for the worst. That meant getting Britain's most precious wealth out of the country, and doing this very fast.

"The destination chosen was British Guiana, as this nation was then known. It was the perfect choice. This was a poor colony, distant from the war—but it had a steady flow of ocean-going freighters, transporting the bauxite that's mined here to make aluminum. Churchill ordered that one very ordinary-looking cargo ship be outfitted for an extraordinary mission.

"That's how a grubby bauxite freighter, the *Vanessa*, came to be steaming across the Atlantic in late 1940. She *looked* as boring as a rusty shipping vessel could look. However, deep down in her hold, lay a cargo unlike any other in history."

Girond takes a breath. The video camera catches his dramatic pause.

Turn to the next page.

"In a specially reinforced cargo area below decks," Girond tells his passengers, "the *Vanessa* carried a treasure almost beyond imagining. At least ten tons of gold bullion, 70 tons of silver, 40 tons of platinum, and 16 million carats of gem-quality diamonds. Total estimated value, in today's dollars: 1.5 *trillion*."

There's a gasp from the businesswoman in the pants suit. The assistant to the silver-haired man has bulging eyes. His boss, so elegant and calm, has fixed a very attentive gaze on Jeremy Girond. But he says nothing.

Go on to the next page.

Your uncle furiously scribbles notes. "That would make this the richest treasure ever found," he mutters without looking up.

"It would indeed," Girond agrees. "And from that day until this, the British government has kept the record of this ship and her mission top secret and sealed. They don't admit that the *Vanessa* existed, not to mention what happened to her. But we...found this."

He waves at the men in blue polo shirts. They tap their keyboards, and one flat-screen monitor flashes to life. On it appears a fuzzy, old, black-and-white photograph of an ocean-going freighter.

"Behold the *Vanessa*," Girond says. "We are the first people to glimpse her photo in more than half a century."

He pauses again, scanning his audience. "Now, let's turn on the underwater cameras—and see how the old girl looks today."

Turn to the next page.

"Before we go on, Mr. Girond—a question."

It's your uncle. He has stopped taking notes. His pen is poised in midair.

"Where did this photograph come from?"

"From old-fashioned research," Girond says. "Before her final mission, the *Vanessa* was registered in the public record, like any commercial freighter."

"May I take a closer look?"

Girond seems to like the drama. "Why not?"

Your uncle walks to the monitor. Chewing thoughtfully on his pen, he examines the blurry image. Then he turns back to Girond.

"So what happened to her?"

The Treasurizers chief shrugs. "Back then in this region, Britain was losing two or three ships per month. The German submarines were very active—and very effective. Because of the secrecy, we may never know which one torpedoed the *Vanessa*.

"But the saddest piece of the story," he says, "may be how near she came to reaching safe harbor. Of course, we're not going to reveal the actual location of our find...but you can tell from the time we've been traveling that we're not too far outside Georgetown harbor.

"That's how close the *Vanessa* was to bringing history's most valuable treasure cargo to safety," Girond says. "Instead, the treasure has lain all these years at the bottom of the sea. And no one has ever admitted that it even exists.

Go on to the next page.

"My friends," Girond says, "all those years of secrecy and loss end...right now."

He snaps his fingers. All the monitors on the wall come to life.

Girond continues to talk about the size of the *Vanessa*'s treasure. He drones on so long about rubies and emeralds and sapphires and gold, you practically fall asleep standing up. But after another fifty minutes or so he winds down. The ROV returns to the mother ship, or at least that's what they explain. And the boat chugs to life and begins to rock and sway, the sign that you are traveling through waves.

Hours later, you return to the hotel. Your uncle is unusually quiet.

"There's something about this that you don't like," you say. "Isn't there?"

His eyes glitter as he glances your way. "Was it obvious?"

"No," you answer—"I just know you. Normally you'd have asked a million questions. But after they shut off the ROV monitors, you hardly said a word."

Turn to the next page.

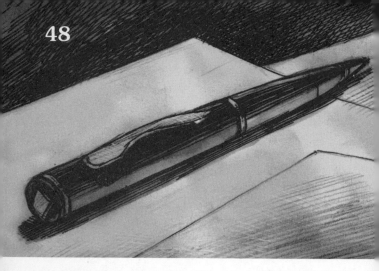

He pulls out his pen. "This isn't just a pen," he says. "It's also a digital camera. See the tiny window?"

You look closely. "Wow," you say. "But why?"

He shrugs. "Treasure hunters are very secretive, as you've seen—but for my books, I have to gather information every way I can. When I went up to look more closely at that fuzzy photo of the supposedly sunken ship, I was really photographing its image on the monitor."

"Okay..."

"Back here, I uploaded the image to some friends at the *Shipping Gazette*, in Britain. That's the journal of the shipping industry there. They've got access to digitized records of every commercial freighter that sailed during World War II. Sure enough, they found our boat."

Go on to the next page.

He turns his laptop around, so you can see. On its screen is the same black-and-white image—of an ordinary-looking old freighter—that Jeremy Girond showed on board *Nemo's Dream*.

But this image isn't fuzzy. It's sharp and clear.

"She was really named the *Carib Sun*," he says. "She was indeed a bauxite freighter, out of British Guiana, and she was indeed sunk by a German U-boat. But she actually went down off the coast of Ireland, in September 1943."

He lets this sink in.

"Wow," you say. "They're lying! This whole story is a fraud."

"But why?"

"Big money," he says. "Jules Whitcomb, that silver-haired gentleman, is a very wealthy investor. That woman in the suit is with Xplore, the cable TV channel. I bet Girond's trying to sell them on a reality TV show. 'Treasure Search.' Something like that."

"That would explain the video cameras," you say.

"Yeah. And if Girond can make himself into a big celebrity, it almost won't matter that the treasure isn't real. In a reality show, they could do anything—make those gold bars mysteriously disappear, for example. Get a whole drama out of *that*."

"I get it," you say. "What should we do?"

A smile spreads across your uncle's face. "Let's beat Girond at his own game."

Turn to the next page.

An hour later, you're at the door of Girond's suite at the Princess Hotel. Your uncle called Girond, asking for an interview, then he spent some time trying to reach Lacey Hastings, the eccentric millionaire, to find out how her trip this morning went. He couldn't get her on the phone, and she wasn't in her room.

"Hmm. Well, I'm sure she'll turn up. Lacey's pretty unpredictable," he says, raising his fist to knock on the door.

Girond is smooth and welcoming, and his suite is very posh. As the two men settle into chairs for their interview, you raise the video camera that your uncle has asked you to operate.

"Mr. Girond," your uncle begins, "I wonder if you've ever heard of a freighter called the *Carib Sun*."

When Girond hears that name, your camera catches the very slight crease that wrinkles his forehead.

Go on to the next page.

Fifteen minutes into his interview with Girond, your uncle has laid out the case for Treasurizers' fantastic discovery being a fake—a scam.

So far, Girond has listened politely, offering no response.

You've got it all on film, including a shot of the sharply focused, black-and-white photo of the *Carib Sun* that your uncle pulled up on his laptop.

"So, Mr. Girond," your uncle finally says. "How do you respond?"

The Treasurizers chief smiles thinly, then, as if he's distracted by something, holds up one finger, and pulls out his cell phone.

"I've got a call coming in," he says. "Do you mind?"

But as you focus closer with the camera lens, you can see he's actually dialing out. Girond punches buttons swiftly. Now he says into the phone: "In here, please."

An inner door opens and the driver Jagad steps into the room, followed by one of the muscular security men.

Girond is very calm. "This gentleman," he says, nodding toward your uncle, "would like to betray our...project. Antoine, put him under wraps. And Jagad, please neutralize this little..."

The driver starts toward you, but your uncle lurches out and knocks him to the floor. Both of Girond's enforcers grab your struggling uncle, who yells: "Run!"

Clutching the video camera, you dash out the door.

Turn to the next page.

You pound down the stairs and push open the door to the hotel's swanky lobby. Girond's enforcers are sure to be heading down in the elevator. You've got just seconds to decide your next move.

You rush up to the check-in counter.

"Jules Whitcomb," you say, casually mentioning the name of the wealthy investor from today's trip. "He's in which room?"

The clerk checks. "Number 312."

"Right."

The guys who'll be coming after you won't be expecting you to go back *up* the hotel stairs. If you can gain entry to Whitcomb's suite, *if* he's there, then Girond won't be able to menace you.

And if anyone can convince Girond to back off and let your uncle go, it'll be the man with the money.

But what if Whitcomb isn't there?

Go on to the next page.

You get a second idea. Somewhere out there is an Internet cafe. If you can find one, and upload your video...you can send it to your parents; they've got lots of connections. Then Girond can't stop the truth from getting seen. He'll no longer have a reason to hold your uncle. You hope.

The indicator above the elevator doors shows what floor the elevator is on. It descends from 2 to 1, to L for lobby. The doors are about to open.

You've got to decide *now*.

If you run upstairs to suite 312,
turn to the next page.

If you try to find an Internet café,
turn to page 57.

No one is in the stairwell. Emerging on the third floor, you see that no one is in the hall.

You listen hard, for footsteps. Nothing.

Quietly and quickly, you pad down the hall.

The wait that follows your quick rap on Jules Whitcomb's door feels like an eternity. Then, in there, you hear footsteps.

You glance behind you once more. The hallway is empty, but now the elevator dings. The door's about to open. Your heart races.

And the door to Suite 312 swings open.

"Well hello, it's you!" says the silver-haired gentleman. "Come on in. Where is your uncle?"

Turn to page 56.

A few hours later, you and your uncle are relaxing, poolside.

You look out on the white clouds that float above the ocean.

"That was really quick thinking," your uncle says, "to go knocking on Jules Whitcomb's door."

He leans back, in the seat next to yours.

You say, "I don't know what would have happened if he hadn't been home."

"But he was. Hey, everything worth doing is a calculated risk," your uncle says. "Girond's whole scheme—the faked treasure, the misidentified shipwreck, the proposal for a TV reality show—it was all a gamble. He knew that. When Whitcomb called him down for a little chat, Girond knew he'd rolled the dice and lost."

"I'm sorry you won't get a book out of all this," you say.

"I still might! I'm thinking of writing my first novel. I might call it *The Treasure Deception*. Catchy title, don't you think?"

The End

You dash out the front door. Several taxis wait outside; you sprint for the nearest one, fling the back door open, and dive onto the seat.

You hear the driver ask, "You okay, man?"

"For now, yeah. Can you get us out of here? *Fast*?"

"You got the right guy!" he says as he stomps on the gas.

The car fishtails away from the Princess Hotel. You peep over the seat; two men come running out through the big front doors. You duck back down.

The driver swerves around a smoke-belching bus, then zooms down the road.

Before long your taxi is well into the city, swallowed up and submerged in a crowd of honking cars, minivans, trucks, motorbikes, and darting bicycles.

You glance above the seat. No sign of pursuers. You let out a long breath, and sit up.

Your driver is a young Indo-Guyanese guy, with silver-rimmed shades and a red racing jacket. He seems pretty cool, and you don't want him to get the wrong impression.

"I...um...didn't do anything bad back there," you say.

He grins. "Hey, everybody's in a hurry these days," he says. "So where you want to go?"

"Do you happen to know a good Internet cafe?"

"Oh sure. *Surf the World!*"

He jerks the wheel hard. You smack into the armrest as the taxi dives down a side lane.

Turn to the next page.

After more twists and turns, you're snaking along a street that's lined with small fruit and vegetable stands, all packed together under a rainbow of colorful, shade-giving umbrellas.

At every stand, tables and wicker baskets are stacked and piled with produce. You glimpse tomatoes, pineapples, oranges, leafy greens, and tropical fruits that you don't recognize at all.

Just beyond the multicolored crowd of stalls, your taxi pulls up and rocks to a stop in front of a pale-gray building with a shiny metal roof. Above its one square window in front, a hand-painted sign says: *Surf the World Cafe*.

Your driver smiles. "Best Internet cafe in Georgetown," he says.

Gratefully, you pay the fare. As you do, he studies you.

"I don't want to get too personal," he says, "but it kind of seems like you got some stress. I could wait around, make sure things are okay. Okay?"

Go on to the next page.

You feel a wave of gratitude. "You know," you say, "that would be good."

On impulse, you stick out your hand, and tell the driver your name. His smile is broad, now.

"Me, I'm Tikram," he says—"but everybody calls me Tiko. I'll wait here. No problem."

The cafe is one long, narrow room, lined with terminals and cooled by rotating fans suspended from a high ceiling. You pay for some time, go sit at a terminal, and log on to your email server.

Your uncle's high-def video minicam has a USB plug that folds out and plugs into your terminal. In minutes, you've uploaded the video to your parents overseas, and to every friend whose email address is saved in your email account.

You glance through the front window. The taxi is out there. It's not one of the newer ones; it's dented and tired-looking. Tiko leans back against the driver's seat in his bright red jacket, one elbow out the open window.

Making a quick decision, you stride for the front door.

Turn to the next page.

You slide back into the taxi—into the front passenger seat this time.

"Tiko," you say, "I'm in a situation."

He was about to start the car. Now he drops his hand, and turns to face you.

"I thought so, the way you needed to get away from that hotel," he says. "What's goin' on?"

You explain everything. Tiko just listens. When you're finally finished, he says, "Those sound like bad guys. Plus they're bad guys with money. The worst kind."

Tiko fishes a cell phone from his jacket pocket. "You got one of these?"

"Sure," you say. "Right here."

"Well, why not use it?"

Go on to the next page.

You're not sure what Tiko means. "Use my phone how?"

"Well, you know this bad guy's name. Right?"

"Yes. Jeremy Girond."

"So call his room. At the hotel. Whoever answers, tell them you've got the video—and unless your uncle walks out that front door in half an hour, you'll be taking it to Channel 6 News."

"Channel 6 News?"

"Sure! *Everyone* in Georgetown watches the news! You say that guy's secretive. So no way does he want that video broadcast."

"Hmm," you say. "It could work."

"Or I could take you to the embassy," Tiko says. "U.S., right? They'll help you out."

*If you go to the U.S. Embassy,
turn to the next page.*

*If you call Jeremy Girond,
turn to page 68.*

Outside the gleaming white gate of the U.S. Embassy, a U.S. Marine stands guard. You've only started to tell him who you are when he holds up his hand, stopping you. He picks up a phone.

"If you'll just hold on a moment," he says.

You're not sure what's happening, but the Marine says into the phone: "Yes. Right here. Okay."

He hangs up. "If you'll come with me, please."

You glance back, at Tiko in his car. You're uncertain, but he nods. You follow the Marine into the large modern building.

You're met in the lobby by a nicely dressed woman who greets you by name. She says, "We are very glad to see you!"

"You are?"

"Oh, we sure are. Will you come with me? Thank you, Corporal," she says to the Marine, who nods sharply before turning and striding back to his post.

In her office, the woman motions for you to sit down. She takes her seat behind a desk.

"I'm Regina Smart, an attaché here at the embassy. And I don't think you realize it, but you've caused quite a stir."

"I have?"

"Oh, yes." She turns to her computer, and taps a few keys.

To your surprise, the image that appears is the first frame of your video. It shows your uncle about to interview Jeremy Girond.

Turn to page 64.

Regina Smart pauses the video. She asks, "Do you know where your uncle is right now?"

"Not for sure," you say. "Do you? And how did you get that video, anyway?"

She smiles. "You emailed it to your parents overseas, yes?"

When you nod, she says, "Well, they got it! And they hopped right on the phone. This video appears to show your uncle being taken hostage. Where did that happen?"

You realize the video doesn't give many clues about its location.

"The Princess Hotel," you say. "That guy Girond has a suite there. My uncle and me..."

But Regina Smart holds up one hand as she grabs her phone with the other.

"We've got a location on that hostage-taking," she says into it. "The Princess Hotel. Uh huh." She looks up at you. "Do you know his room number?"

"Uh...I'm not sure..."

"That's okay. *Girond*," she says into the phone.

"The company's called Treasurizers," you add.

She passes that info along. Then she hangs up.

"A police team is on its way," she tells you. "If your uncle is still in that hotel, they'll find him."

"What if he's not?"

She looks thoughtful. "Do you know where they might have taken him?"

Go on to the next page.

"No. What if they hurt him or something?"

"Well...let's just sit tight, for now. Sometimes," she adds with a thin smile, "the waiting is the hardest part."

She's sure right about that.

Through the slow agony of waiting, the hands on Regina Smart's wall clock hardly ever seem to move. Minute after minute crawls by, until...somehow...a little more than an hour has passed.

Regina Smart is busy at her computer.

You're just sitting there, staring at the clock.

Turn to the next page.

66

At last her phone rings. She answers.

"Yes? Oh, good. Right. Okay."

She hangs up—and your heart leaps to see the expression on her face.

"They found him," she says. "He was still in that suite."

"Is he..."

"He's fine," she says. "Girond and his men are under arrest. They didn't put up a fight. I think once you got away from the hotel with that video, Girond knew the game was up. It was only a matter of time.

"Trouble is," she adds, "taking an American citizen hostage—that's a serious offense. He probably wishes he'd stopped at scamming money from rich people who thought they were funding a treasure hunt. When his scheme got exposed, he panicked and went too far."

"There's one thing I don't understand," you say.

"What's that?"

Go on to the next page.

"Well," you say, "Treasurizers really did find a shipwreck. We saw it through their underwater cameras. It did get torpedoed, too. The cameras showed a jagged hole in its hull."

Regina Smart nods. "So many ships went to the bottom, in that war," she says. "Who knows how many men went down with them? It was a terrible time."

"Yeah, but...I mean," you say, "so Treasurizers did find a wreck. And they did have this cool boat, with high-tech treasure-hunting equipment. So, like, was that all a fake, or what?"

She shrugs. "Maybe they *were* chasing a real mystery. Maybe there really was a treasure ship, disguised as a British freighter. Maybe Girond's people tried to find it but couldn't. Treasure hunting is very, very expensive. There's huge pressure to come up with a valuable find."

"So," you speculate, "maybe Girond got desperate, and cooked up this scheme?"

"It's possible. Or else he might have planned this all along. If he had secured the financial backing *and* the TV show, he could have pulled in millions. Eventually he might have said, 'Oh well, we *thought* we'd find treasure. Sorry.'

"In a way," she adds, "he's a kind of pirate."

"A pirate?"

"Sure. He's roaming the seas, looking to steal treasure and find fame. I think your uncle might get a good book out of this after all."

Her phone rings again. She answers, and smiles.

"Your uncle's here," she says.

You go rushing for the front door.

The End

The hotel puts you through to Girond's suite.

"Who is this?" says the man who answers the call.

"Mr. Girond?"

He repeats: "Who is this?" It's a gruff voice—not the smooth Girond.

"Please tell Mr. Girond that I've got the video," you say. "Unless he lets my uncle walk out the front door of the hotel in half an hour, I'm taking it to Channel 6 News."

"Hold on," the gruff voice says. You hear some voices, muffled in the background.

"All right," the same voice says. "Here's a better offer: you bring us that video in half an hour or less. Or your uncle dies."

"What? No."

But the phone has gone dead.

By now it's late in the day: what might, back home, be called rush hour. The street on the way back to the hotel is jammed with minivans, motorbikes, cars, and trucks. Tiko dodges through as fast as he can, darting into openings that look too small for his car.

Even so, it takes you almost twenty nerve-wracking minutes to reach the Princess Hotel.

Finally the high, broad, glittery shape of the hotel appears ahead.

As you come closer, Tiko says, "Hey, man. You see what I see?"

You do see it. For some reason, the driveway out in front of the hotel is filled with police cars.

Turn to page 70.

A little over a year later, your uncle's first book for young adults appears in stores. It's called <u>The Treasure Ship Scam</u>, and it's the first fictional book he's written. It stars a young American who, with help from a resourceful taxi driver, a video camera, and a cell phone, plays the key role in exposing and stopping an elaborate moneymaking scheme.

According to the novel, a group of international scammers, led by a very smooth, well-dressed man named Rodrigo Merej, were aiming to rake in millions of dollars, searching for the lost treasure of a top secret treasure ship. It's a ship that may, in fact, never have existed at all.

"That is *quite* a plot," a perky TV interviewer says to your uncle as he begins his promotional tour for the new book. "How did you ever dream up a story like that?" she asks.

Your uncle smiles. For a moment, he looks into the camera, as if he and someone out there are sharing a secret.

"I didn't create the plot all by myself," he says.

"Oh no?"

"No. The truth is," he tells the interviewer, "I had a little help."

The End

"Okay," you say to the boy with the dreadlocks. "Let's go."

The man from Treasurizers is shocked—and upset.

"Don't be foolish!" he says. "This person is a street hustler!"

"That's what I'm afraid of," your uncle whispers to you. "But okay. Let's go."

As you follow the boy out of the terminal, you look back to see the Treasurizers guy talking into a cell phone. Then you step outside into the heat-blasting sun, the blaring of taxi horns, the wheezing of buses pulling up, and the overhead roar of a jet taking off.

Turn to the next page.

The boy leads you to a small blue minibus. It's packed with people. Your uncle says, "How can we fit?"

"No problem!" says the boy. He hops on, and beckons to you.

Some people shift to the back. Now you, your uncle, his suitcase, your backpack, and your young guide all squeeze onto the bench seat behind the driver. The seats in back of you are even more jammed than they were before.

"Guess we're going to see Georgetown local style," your uncle says.

Neither of you sees the dark-blue sedan that pulls out behind the minivan. As the driver from Treasurizers begins to follow your vehicle, he stays a careful distance behind.

Turn to page 74.

Georgetown is full of old-time white buildings, some really fancy and cool looking. But the bus keeps going, into a neighborhood where the wooden homes get more and more run down. Then, up ahead, you spot water.

"Are we close to the harbor?" your uncle asks.

"Yes!" says the boy.

You ask, "Who are we going to see?"

He lowers his head, and whispers: "Too many people listenin' just now. In Guyana we got a saying: *Mouth open, story jump out.*"

"What's that mean?"

"It means nobody can keep a secret!"

He tosses his dreadlocks, and grins. He asks you for your name, and you tell him. Then you say, "What's yours?"

He gives you a look. "My name is Waverly," he admits, "but you better not call me that."

"Why not?"

"'Cause I don' like it! Everybody calls me Wave," he says, smiling now.

You step out of the minibus onto a street that's crammed with narrow, open-front shops. Rickety tables outside the shops are piled with stuff for sale, from sunglasses to electric blenders. Signs above the shops shout out names in bright colors: "*Breeze!*" and "*Misty*" and "*Blast!*"

"This way," Wave says.

He leads you down a narrow, dusty lane. You walk several blocks through shadowy alleys.

Go on to the next page.

"In here," says Wave as he ducks into the windowless building facing the ship. It's like an airplane hangar, with one big opening in front.

It's cooler inside the building, out of the sun. From here out to the ship, workers are hefting sacks and wheeling wooden crates. This is a warehouse—a loading depot.

Over in a corner, in gloomy shadows, the boy leads you toward someone sitting on a folding chair. As your eyes adjust, you see he's an older man, slender and white haired. He sits very straight, watching you come.

"This is my granddaddy," Wave says. "He is a sailing man."

"Granddaddy," Wave says to the gentleman, "these folks come 'bout the treasure ship."

The man extends his hand with formal politeness. "I am Winston Crawford," he says. "I see you've met my Waverly.

"Please," he says, pulling out two more folding chairs. "Sit."

As you sit beside him, Winston gazes out the big door. Through it, beyond the cargo ship, you see shimmering water.

Winston glances around, to make sure no one else is listening.

"I will tell you a story. You will find it difficult to believe."

Turn to the next page.

The tale Winston Crawford tells is definitely strange. Last week a shrimp boat left the harbor, on a day's normal run after the "seabob" and "white belly" shrimp that are, he explains, plentiful off Guyana's shore.

Winston's eyes flare.

"And what happens? Some guys blaze up on a speedboat and pull out guns. *Guns*! They tell the shrimpers, 'You got two choices. Either we kill you right here, or we give you good money. Real good money. All you have to do for this money is go back to Georgetown, and tell everyone you saw this weird purple mist.'"

Your uncle says, "Purple *mist*?"

Winston nods. "They said, 'Tell people this mist came over your boat. Then tell them inside the mist was the ghost of an old-time pirate ship. Say you saw this ghost ship! Tell *everyone*. Say you're too scared ever to go back out to that place again.'

"Then these guys say, 'If you tell anyone the *truth*, we will hear about it. 'Cause we got people in this harbor, okay? We got people working for us. So if you tell anyone 'bout this *real* boat, and these real guns, we will come after you. And your families.'

"They said, 'We are not fooling around, we got a big-money thing goin' on here. So you go tell everyone 'bout that purple mist. Here's the money. You want it?'"

Your uncle says, "Did they take it?"

Winston shrugs. "They are poor fishermen. Sure they took it."

Turn to page 78.

"So," Winston Crawford says, "the shrimp men came back here and told everyone about this mysterious mist, and this ghost pirate ship, and everyone believes it. People *like* stories, and this is a good one."

Wave, beside you, is angry now. "People around here are too superstitious," he says. "They're all sayin' it's a *jumbie* ship."

"A what?"

"A ship full of ghosts. Jumbies," he says.

"That's right," Winston agrees. "And every time somebody tells this story, it gets more colorful. Now folks tell you that the shrimpers saw old-time pirates coming out of that ship, with pistols and daggers. If you ask the shrimpers themselves about that, they just smile.

"But I don't believe this," the old sailor says. "I been on the water all my life—and there's no purple mist. So I bring one of those shrimpers in here. I feed him a little rum. I feed him more rum. Finally, he tells me the truth."

Winston sits back, crosses his arms.

"But," your uncle asks, "who *were* those guys in the speedboat?"

"They got to be the same people say they found a big treasure out there," Winston says, nodding at the water. "Those people have been throwing money around this harbor. Hiring folks to be bodyguards and drivers and all. *Got* to be them."

"But why would Treasurizers want to spread a story about a mist?"

Go on to the next page.

The old sailor lifts his eyebrows. "You're the writer. Go find out."

"My granddaddy's got lots more stories," Wave says. "He was in the war—in the Merchant Navy."

"Is *that* right?" your uncle says. Winston nods.

"The Merchant Navy was Britain's service for running those freighters," your uncle explains to you. To Winston, he says: "This sunken ship is supposed to be from the war."

"I know about all the ships from that time," the old sailor says.

Your uncle takes out his notebook. "I'd love to hear more," he says. "Mr. Crawford, may I buy you a cold drink?"

The old sailor nods. "A cafe next door sells good Guyanese ginger beer. Waverly can go get some."

"No—I'd like to do it," your uncle says. "Look around just a little. You stay here," he tells you, "okay? I'll be right back."

You enjoy chatting with Wave and his grandaddy —but a minute later, there's a commotion outside. You hear shouts. One sounds like your uncle. Leaping up, you hear squealing tires.

You run out onto the boardwalk alone. The workmen are upset.

"That man you were with," one says—"this man stopped and grabbed him!"

"*Grabbed* him?" you say. "How?"

Turn to the next page.

"He had a gun. It happened very fast," another workman says.

Trying hard to stay calm, you ask: "What did he look like?"

"He was Indo-Guyanese," the man says—"dark hair, dark suit."

"They went in a blue car," says a third. He makes a snaking motion with his hand, like a car swerving away. "They're gone!"

Shaken, you repeat the story to Wave and his grandfather.

"What's *Indo-Guyanese* mean?"

"Half of the people in Guyana come from India —or their grandparents did," Winston says. "They came years ago, under the British. For work."

Something clicks. "That guy in the airport," you say to Wave.

"He was Indo-Guyanese," he says. "And he had on a dark suit!"

What else do you know? There must be something.

Go on to the next page.

"We can call the police," Winston says, "but they probably won't be much help. Not unless you offer them money."

Money. It hits you: you hardly have any. Just a $20 bill in your pocket.

Then you remember something.

"The Princess Hotel!" you say. "That guy said he wanted to take us to the Princess Hotel. Is that a real place?"

"Yes—most famous hotel in Georgetown," Winston says. "If the treasure hunters are spending a lot of money, they would be staying there. It could be their headquarters."

"How do I get there?"

"Waverly could take you," the old man says— "but I don't think you should go. These people are kidnappers, we know this much. Stay here. Do you have a phone?"

"Sure."

"Sometimes patience is best," he advises. "Wait and see if it rings. Why show yourself? Just wait."

You don't want to. But he might be right.

If you go to the Princess Hotel,
turn to the next page.

If you wait for a call, turn to page 94.

"I have \$20—American money," you say to Wave. "Will that get us to the hotel?"

He whistles. "Around here that's a lot. Give it to me, okay?"

"What?"

"I will change it for you. Just wait."

Trusting your new friend, you hand him the bill. Five minutes later, he's back. He hands you a wad of strange bills.

"Four thousand Guyanese dollars," Wave says, counting.

"Four *thousand*?"

"That's what \$20 U.S. is worth. Come on."

Back up the alleys to the street full of shops, you two hop on a minibus. It's as jammed as the last one. Just as it pulls away, your cell phone buzzes.

"It's me," your uncle says. "I'm okay. I'm in the Princess Hotel. You won't believe this! They want me to host a reality TV show."

"*What*?"

"I know, it sounds crazy," he says. "But I can explain. I think."

"Start with why they grabbed you—with a *gun*," you say.

"Oh, that driver just overreacted," your uncle says. "They told him to bring me to them at this hotel. I guess you don't say no to this Treasurizers guy. The driver was afraid he'd get fired, or maybe worse—so he made sure I came with him. It looked worse than it really was."

"Well, I don't like this," you say. "What do they mean, a *reality* show?"

Go on to the next page.

"They'll call their show *Treasure of the Pirate Mist*," your uncle explains. "I think that's why they created the rumor about this ghostly mist—it'll sound great on TV. They'll do the show about searching for a secret lost treasure ship. But out on the water, suddenly a purple mist will cover everything. It'll be a huge plot twist."

"Doesn't sound like a *reality* show," you say.

"Have you watched those shows? *None* of them are about reality! This could be a big break for me—I've never been on TV," he says. "They're even offering you a part, working on the salvage ship. Come to the hotel. Let's be on TV together."

"But these people pulled a gun on you," you point out. "And they threatened to kill those fishermen."

"They are a little intense," he agrees. "But I don't like us being apart, you and me."

"I'll be okay with Winston and Wave. He and I could nose around the harbor a little. We can ask what else people have heard about Treasurizers."

"That might get dangerous," your uncle says.

"Hey, *you're* with the people who've got guns."

"All right," your uncle says. "I leave it up to you! But I really thought you'd want to be on TV with me!"

---

*If you go to join your uncle and the TV Project,
turn to the next page.*

*If you stay to learn what you can at the harbor,
turn to page 86.*

Three months later, standing under a hot sun out on the ocean, you look over the rail of the high-tech salvage ship *Nemo's Dream*. Video cameras build the breath-holding suspense as you and a crowd of other crew members peer into the deep waters. You're all waiting for the ship's remote-operated diving vessel to surface.

Down there, clutched in one robot claw of the ROV, is a rectangular object. It's silvery metal, about eight inches long. It's called an ingot. And down below are hundreds more.

Hundreds.

Your uncle strides out from inside the ship. Just like you, he's wearing a blue polo shirt with the logo of Treasurizers, Inc. He's the host of this reality TV show, *Treasure of the Pirate Mist*. Following him is Jeremy Girond, the slick and calculating chief of Treasurizers.

"This has to be the most exciting and intense moment in a treasure-hunter's life," your uncle says to Girond. "Are these bars what we think they are?"

Girond shrugs. He actually looks confused—like he never expected this to happen.

"I...I don't know," he says.

Then he seems to remember the TV cameras that are recording every word.

"It's a fantastic development," he says to them.

If Jeremy Girond was shocked to spot the incredible sight that appeared on his ship's underwater camera monitors just a little while ago, he couldn't have been more surprised than you.

Go on to the next page.

Over these weeks of working on this ship, you've grown very skeptical of Treasurizers, Inc.

There's no treasure at all, you've been thinking. *This is all about building up drama. It's just an act for television.*

Treasurizers has sent its ROV down to explore the sunken World War II freighter that lies deep below *Nemo's Dream*. Girond told the cameras that on an earlier dive, the cameras on his ROV spotted a stack of gold bars outside the wreck.

But later, those bars had somehow mysteriously disappeared.

That's when you started getting suspicious.

The missing gold bars became one episode of *Treasure of the Pirate Mist*, Treasurizers' new show on the Xplore cable channel. Girond and his people also built episodes around the strange purple mist that seemed to spout up from the water, near the ship, whenever the show's action lagged. Special-effects experts altered the videos of that mist, to make the ghostly image of an old-time sailing ship seem to float within it.

That's when you were sure this whole project was a fake.

Then today Girond's crew took a risky step. They decided to send their ROV through the jagged torpedo wound in the hull of the sunken freighter.

They were going to look inside the ship.

Turn to page 130.

Winston has reservations about you two nosing around the harbor, but his grandson is as curious as you are. Reluctantly, Winston agrees to let you investigate.

That's how you come to be inside a dim, back-street café near the waterfront. You and Waverly drink ginger sodas as you try to draw more information out of the shrimp fisherman who confessed the truth to Wave's grandfather.

Today there's terror in his eyes.

"There was a mist—really," he insists. "And pirates!"

You don't argue. Instead you ask, "Who were those people? Have you seen them around?"

He nods. "Jonah Martin," he says to Wave. "You know him?"

"Sure. Big man. Works at the wharf some-times," Wave says.

"That's him. He's some kind of guard for them. I don't know where, but he works at night," the man says. "Please—I can't say no more! They threatened my *family*."

Wave nods. "We'll go," he says. "We never saw you here. No one will know."

"Good boy," the fisherman says. "Just like your granddaddy."

"That's the only reason he talked to me," Wave tells you as you walk outside. "Everyone around here has so much respect for Winston Crawford."

"So what should we do?"

Go on to the next page.

"I know where that guy Jonah hangs out," he says, "he's got a room near here. If he works for those people at night, let's watch and see where he goes."

As the evening deepens into night by the waterfront, no one pays attention to two loitering young people.

"Hey, it's no big deal," Wave says. "We just limin'."

"What's *limin'*?"

"Hangin' 'round. People do it all the time, 'round here," he says.

To blend in, he insists that you buy a typical Guyana T-shirt. The one he chooses has the logo of a Florida baseball team.

"Now you look local," he said.

"How can *this* be local?"

He shrugs. "People here like American things."

"Do you even know what sport they play?" you ask.

"It's not cricket," he says. "Right?"

"Cricket? No."

"If it's not cricket, then I don't care what it is. Cricket is the *only* game."

Wave heads down an alley. You shrug, and follow.

You two are hanging around, keeping an eye on the front door of the building where Jonah Martin lives.

Turn to the next page.

A text message comes into your phone. It's from your uncle:

We ID'd a Treasurizers security guard,

you reply.

We're watching to see where he goes.
My gosh. Be Careful!

Beefy Jonah Martin comes out wearing a black T-shirt and black jeans. He blends into the night. Wave whispers, "Just walk natural."

"What if he sees us?"

"No problem. We're just kids."

You saunter some distance behind Jonah as he walks through streets and lanes until he comes out at another section of the waterfront. This area is modern looking, with large warehouses inside security fences, and stacks of huge metal shipping containers.

Go on to the next page.

Docked along the water, you can see the looming shapes of large freighters.

Jonah stops at a smaller vessel, berthed along the cobblestoned dockside. It's modern looking, but it's not a freighter. Atop its squarish midship structure is a little forest of high-tech antennas.

This must be the Treasurizers salvage vessel—the one they'll use to search for the underwater treasure. That boat must have valuable equipment inside. You can see why Treasurizers would hire a guard.

Suddenly there's a loud rattling, an all-piercing racket. Startled, frightened, you shrink against a tall security fence.

"What's *that*?"

Wave pokes his head out, to look. He turns back grinning.

"It's just some drummin' and dancin'! Go ahead. Take a look."

Turn to the next page.

Out there, about 50 feet across the cobblestones from the Treasurizers vessel, three young men wearing backwards baseball caps have started playing drums. They're pounding and clattering with drumsticks, on two snares and a deeper tom tom, making a storm of rhythms.

Two other boys are dancing. They're incredible too—deft, creative, and wild.

You ask Wave, "Does this just *happen*?"

He shrugs. "Sure. But...this is a funny place for it. See, now—Jonah don't like it."

Looking stern, the security guard strides toward the five young men. He says to them, in accented English, "Hey, maan—you caan' be playin' that stuff here!"

The young men stop. Obediently, they set down their drumsticks. They reach into the big pockets of their cargo shorts, and pull out pistols.

"So now we do this," one of the men says to Jonah. "Lie down on the ground."

Wave's eyes are wide. He jerks his head toward the darkness, the wordless signal to run. But your cell phone buzzes. Your uncle's texting:

Where are you?

The young men with guns and backwards caps are walking toward the Treasurizers ship. One is using duct tape to tie up Jonah Martin on the ground.

You could text your uncle, so he can warn Treasurizers. Or you could just run for it.

If you send a warning, go on to the next page.

If you run for safety, turn to page 93.

No one has seen you. The robbers are warily approaching the boat, guns drawn.

Very quietly, you text:

The answer comes quickly:

Turn to the next page.

No. They don't see us.

Get out of there! I will sound alarm.

You hang up. But the few seconds you've taken have been critical.

Inside the Treasurizers boat is a second guard, this one heavily armed. Seeing five men with pistols approaching, he radios for help. Then he takes aggressive, panicky action.

At the moment you and Wave turn to run, the guard shoves open a window and lets loose a barrage of automatic weapon fire. Shooting wildly at the approaching men, he spots your retreating figure and assumes you're with the attackers.

He unleashes another burst. Bullets career up the passageway. Wave has dashed up ahead; but two of the bullets catch you in the back.

Five minutes after the guard drives the attackers off, sirens come howling toward the harbor. By the time they reach the dock near the Treasurizers salvage vessel, two people lie badly wounded on the cobblestones.

One other has managed to escape, as has Waverly Crawford.

Three people, the police find, are dead. One is younger than the others, wears a bloodstained T-shirt with the logo of a Florida baseball team.

The End

"Boy, am I glad you got out of there," your uncle says, back home in his apartment. "You could have got caught in the gun battle, when the guard inside the boat started firing on that gang."

You sigh. This is a conversation you two have had a dozen times. When will your uncle let it go?

"Hey," you say, "we got home okay."

"Yeah. That robbery attempt was the last straw," your uncle says. "I went down to research a treasure hunt, but all we saw were guns. I'm not really into guns."

You glance at the old pirate pistol on his display shelf. "Okay," you say—"can I have that one?"

"Of course you can't! Anyway, that's a *history* gun. I don't like *reality* guns."

"Well," you say, "I'm just sorry you didn't get a new book out of the whole thing."

"I'm not sorry at all. Imagine how I would have felt if you'd been killed."

"How would *you* have felt? How about me? Oh wait," you say. "I'd have been dead."

"And that's not the ending to any story I'd ever want to write," your uncle says.

In your pocket, your cell phone buzzes. It's your buddy Wave, from Georgetown.

You say to your uncle, "Can we talk about this later?"

"No," he says, "I think we've talked about it enough. End of story."

Well, THAT's a relief, you think as you answer your phone.

"Yo, Waverly!"

The End

A half hour later, your phone buzzes.

"It's me," your uncle says. "I'm okay. I'm checked in at the Princess Hotel."

"The guys on the dock said you were kidnapped!"

"Oh, that driver guy overreacted," your uncle says. "The Treasurizers told him to bring me to them at this hotel. This driver just takes his job very seriously. It looked worse than it was."

You consider this.

"It still seems weird to me," you admit.

"It is, a little," your uncle agrees. "First off, how did they know I was coming? I told a few friends and associates in the treasure-hunting world, but I didn't make a public announcement."

"Yeah, but you're a well-known writer and you write about treasure hunting," you say. "Rumor could have spread that you were coming."

"I guess so," your uncle says. "But why would that driver be so scared of the Treasurizers guy? His name is Girond, by the way. Jeremy Girond."

"The driver?"

"No, the top guy of Treasurizers. He welcomed me into the hotel," your uncle says. "He's a very smooth talker, but he's got these two thug-like bodyguards, and the driver was clearly petrified of him. In fact...uh oh, wait. I better call you back."

The phone goes dead.

Go on to the next page.

This wait is even more harrowing than the last one. When the phone finally buzzes, you seize it.

"Are you all right?"

"I'm fine," your uncle says. "Girond came by the room to ask me to go out on their salvage vessel tomorrow morning. He also told me they are filming the trip. He's thinking of doing a television show about treasure hunting."

"Well...that could be popular," you speculate.

"Yeah, it could. And get this—they want me to be the host!"

"Wow. Would you *do* that?"

"I don't know," your uncle says. "It would mean good money, and a terrific promotion for my books. But this guy Girond...there's something about him I don't like. Why all the security? Why was that driver so scared of messing up? Anyway, guess what? He thinks I came alone."

"What do you mean?"

"Like I said, his driver panicked and just grabbed me," your uncle explains. "When we got here, I think the driver didn't want to admit to Girond that there are actually *two* of us here, since he only produced one. So he said nothing about you. Girond assumes I'm here alone.

"So, basically," your uncle adds, "you're a free agent. I'm thinking you're in a good position to find out some things from the outside, while I try to learn more from the inside."

"I can do that. But how?"

Turn to the next page.

"Well, right now we've got two good allies—two people who will help us," your uncle says. "Winston knows everyone on the waterfront, and he's well-respected. His grandson's got spirit. He's smart and resourceful. Do you think you can stay with them, for now?"

"I think so. That would be fun."

"Good. See what you can find out. Talk to people on the waterfront. But be really careful!"

"Don't worry."

In your pocket, you've got only $20 U.S., but that turns out to be worth enough in Guyanese dollars that you're all right, for now. And the Crawfords are happy to take care of you.

After a night in their tidy cottage near the water, eating spicy Guyanese food and listening to Winston Crawford's amazing stories of the sea, Wave and you spend a full day combing the waterfront, chatting casually with people. You hear all sorts of rumors.

One is that Treasurizers, Inc. actually has *three* boats: their well-equipped salvage vessel, plus a powerful speedboat, and a mini-submarine. Men armed with automatic weapons are said to be going out in the speedboat, patrolling the area where Treasurizers aims to mount their undersea salvage operation.

That makes sense, in a way. You've learned how secretive and protective treasure hunters can be about their finds. But what's the purpose of the sub? For now, that's a mystery. It could be just a rumor.

Then your uncle calls.

Turn to page 98.

"I've found some *interesting* information," he says.

"You remember," he says, "that I told you Treasurizers claims they've found a sunken freighter that was secretly transporting a huge fortune? It was supposedly carrying gold, silver, and diamonds out of England at the darkest time of World War II, in 1940."

"Right," you say. "It was headed for Georgetown, but it got torpedoed offshore by a German U-boat."

"But get this," he says. "Today they produced a blurry, black-and-white photo of this freighter and I secretly photographed it. I sent the image to my contacts in the shipping industry. They found the same photograph in the historical archives. It was a British freighter all right, and it was sunk by a U-boat—but off the coast of Ireland. In 1943!"

"What?"

"Yeah," he says. "When Treasurizers took us out to their shipwreck site today, they kept us below decks so we couldn't guess the location. On monitors, they showed us some live images of gold bars on the ocean floor. But I could tell they weren't real gold."

"How?"

Go on to the next page.

"I'll explain later," he says. "Listen, I ran into a friend at the hotel, a wealthy American treasure enthusiast named Lacey Hastings. She's got a fast yacht with all the high-tech toys. She says she's figured out where this secret shipwreck site is. She wanted to take her boat out there today, but I convinced her to wait."

"Okay..."

"She's coming to meet you," he says. "Where is the Crawfords' home exactly?"

You consider the off-the-map location.

"Tell her I will meet her at the Moth Café," you say. "And lead her over to Winston's house."

"Great!" says your uncle. He hangs up quickly. You can tell the stories are already whirring in the writer's mind.

Turn to the next page.

An hour later, you, Wave and Lacey Hastings are sitting in wicker rocking chairs on the front porch of Winston Crawford's small, tidy white house.

You've just told them about your uncle's call. Lacey shakes her head.

"I *knew* it," she says. "Something never felt right about this Jeremy Girond character. So is he a crook, a pirate, a con-man, or what?"

"My uncle thinks it's all about getting a TV reality series," you say. "He says if Girond can get a TV show about searching for treasure, he can make millions whether they find any or not."

"Absolutely true," Lacey says. "A brilliant plan, in a way."

Her eyes are shining.

"So let's destroy it," she says. "I think we three can be a great team."

"Sure," says Wave. "But how?"

Lacey smacks one hand against the other. "*Ideas*! We need ideas, people!"

"I've got one," you say.

"Me too," says Wave.

"Right," says Lacey. "Let's hear 'em."

Turn to page 102.

102

"You go first," Lacey says to you.

"Okay," you say. "So we've collected lots of information, and some might be true or might be rumors—like this weird business about the purple mist. But my uncle has proof that the shipwreck isn't what they say it is. He also says he knows the gold bars, which they supposedly found on the ocean floor, aren't real."

"Right. So..."

"So we make a Web site! *The Truth About Treasurizers*. We photograph their vessel, we put up the info my uncle found...we put up everything we can. My uncle's got contacts with everyone in the worldwide treasure-hunting community. All kinds of people will visit the site, and the Treasurizers guy won't know *where* it's coming from. It'll drive him crazy! And it'll get the truth out there."

"It sure would," says Lacey. "And I've got broadband Internet here on the boat. Wave, what's your idea?"

"Mine's about *this* community," he says. "The people who are here on the waterfront are hardworking, and they're very superstitious. When that rich man came around spreading this stuff about purple mist and pirates, people here believed it right away they thought it was a jumbie ship.

"Now we look like fools," he says fiercely— "and now fishermen think it's not safe to go out to the good shrimping grounds no more. So their families are hurtin'.

"It's not right," Wave adds—"and it's not *true*. Let's show everyone the truth."

Go on to the next page.

"Okay," says Lacey. "How?"

"Everyone trusts me," Wave says. "And if not me, my grandpa. If we took them out to the shrimping grounds to show them it was safe, they'd follow us."

"Makes sense," Lacey says.

"But we don't have a boat anymore," Wave says. He looks around the yacht and smiles. "Maybe we could lead them out to sea on yours?"

Lacey nods. "I would do that," she says.

You ask, "What if Treasurizers tries to stop you?"

"They threatened one little boat full of shrimpers," Wave says. "What they gonna do if ten or twenty boats come out there?"

Lacey is silent now, thinking. Finally she says, "Wave, I love your idea, but I'm part of the world community of treasure-fanciers. I want them to know the truth. I vote for the Web site."

They both turn to you. "Looks like you're the deciding vote," Lacey says.

"Actually," you admit, "I like Wave's idea as much as mine. Truth boats!"

Lacey shouts, "That is no help!"

She winks at Wave. Those two are becoming real friends.

"You got to make the pick," Wave says.

If you vote to create a truth-telling Web site, turn to the next page.

If you vote to organize a flotilla of "truth boats," turn to page 110.

Using your laptop on Lacey's broadband Internet connection, you create the website *The Truth About Treasurizers*. Your uncle sends the URL, or Web address, to his international contact list.

You post photos you've snapped of the Treasurizers vessel, *Nemo's Dream*, using a miniature spy camera that's one of Lacey's many toys. You write about the rumor—the purple mist and ghost pirate ship—that has swept the Georgetown harbor. Wave writes an impassioned blog post under an anonymous account.

"Superstition isn't truth!" he declares. "We're digging out the true story! Keep visiting this site!"

In just a few days, hundreds, then thousands, of people do just that. Your uncle pretends to cooperate with Jeremy Girond of Treasurizers, but he reports to you that Girond is furious. "He's trying to be cool," your uncle says. "But I think he's getting desperate."

You wait a few days for your big reveal: the blurry photo that Girond says is a war-era photograph of the wrecked treasure ship. Alongside it, you post the clear version of the same photo, emailed to your uncle by a shipping journal in England. That's the "smoking gun," proving that Girond's "discovery" is a fraud.

But it also tells Girond that an insider is behind the Web site.

Go on to the next page.

You get a phone call just a few hours after the big reveal.

"I've been arrested," your uncle says.

"*Arrested*? What happened?"

"Apparently," he explains, "Girond has very powerful friends in Guyana. They want his show to go forward. It could bring lots of money into this country. They're saying if I don't shut down the Web site, they'll prosecute me for slander. I could go to prison. At least, that's the threat."

"But," you ask, "how did they connect you to the Web site?"

"Treasurizers only showed that blurry photo to four people." Your uncle gulps. "Two of them vanished immediately after the Web site is posted. They somehow narrowed it down to me."

"Girond wants the Web site shut down, obviously, but I want to get a good book out of this," your uncle says. "I'm not afraid to go to jail! Well, maybe I am a little. The jails in Guyana are supposed to be pretty bad."

He takes a breath. You can tell he is a little frightened. You would be, too.

Turn to the next page.

"Anyway," he says, "this whole thing about jail might be just a threat. And you could tell people—all my contacts—what's happened. You could raise a ruckus!"

"With the Web site, I really could," you say.

"Right. So that's the choice," he says. "Only you can make it, I'm afraid. We either keep the Web site going, and find out how real this threat of jail is or we shut the site down. If we do that, we'll still have our information. And we can keep on investigating."

"Girond still doesn't know I'm here," you remind your uncle. "If there are changes to the Web site while you are in prison, he'll know you have an accomplice."

"True," your uncle says. "You'll need to be very careful."

You think, just for a moment. You know you need to decide quickly, while your uncle's still on the line.

If you shut down the Web site but keep the investigation going, go on to the next page.

If you defy Girond's threat, risking prison for your uncle, turn to page 109.

You agree to shut down the site. Wave helps you remove everything you've uploaded and completely erase the Web site. But then your uncle isn't just released.

He's deported.

"I can only talk for a second," he says on your cell phone. "I'm in the airport—I just went through security. They're putting me on a plane home in half an hour. It's all happened very fast. I guess Girond wants me out of the country."

"I'm gonna get this jerk," you say. "Once you're safe at home, the site goes back up."

"That actually won't be necessary," he says. "Girond's investors have all pulled out. We wrecked his whole scheme—but now I'm worried about you. Are you still with Lacey?"

"I'm still staying with the Crawfords, but Lacey is buying us groceries and stuff," you say. "We meet every day, to work on our project."

"Please tell her she needs to get you out of the country as soon as possible," he says. "I'm afraid Girond and his thugs may be closing in. They know I had help. They've got people in their pay, down at the harbor.

"Tell Lacey I'll pay her back," he adds "but please, ask her to get you on a plane home. Tonight, if possible."

Lacey does that—and more.

Turn to the next page.

108

Not only does she get you on a Caribbean Airlines flight out of Georgetown that evening, she hires a limousine to drive you to the airport.

"Nobody's going to hassle a limo," she says.

That turns out to be true. When you board the plane, you discover you've got a first-class seat.

Not bad, you think as you stretch out.

Once you're safely home, Lacey arranges for Waverly Crawford to attend a first-class private school in the U.S., all costs paid.

During Wave's vacations, Lacey flies him *and* you to Georgetown. You stay in Winston Crawford's cottage, and the four of you reminisce about the time you took down an international fraud attempt.

Winston tells a lot more stories. In fact, he has so many great tales, from all his years as a merchant seaman, that you start filming them, using Lacey's high-def minicam.

You start posting Winston Crawford's tales on YouTube. Before long, the old sailor is a global Internet sensation.

"What'll *you* do next?" Wave asks you, during one vacation.

"I'm thinking of creating a show for the Net," you say. "*Guyana—the Last Paradise*. Your granddaddy can be our guest celebrity. I'll need a great host."

He tosses his dreadlocks and grins. "I can only do it during vacations. I'm very busy."

"Well, me too."

"So let's get started!"

The End

On your site's home page, you post a huge banner headline:

GUYANA JAILS NOTED TREASURE-HUNT AUTHOR! TREASURIZERS, INC. WANTS THIS SITE SHUT DOWN

The reaction is immediate. The *Guyana News* adapts what you've written, adding some vague quotes from police officials, into a front-page story. This is picked up by the Associated Press, and the online news article goes out around the world.

A couple of tense days later, you haven't heard a word from your uncle. Then your phone rings. Your heart lifts to hear your uncle's voice.

"The New York Times sent a reporter down to Georgetown," he says. "That was the last straw. Girond knew he couldn't fool or bully people any longer. They let me out of jail an hour ago."

"How was it?"

"Not so bad."

"What about Girond?"

"He's left Guyana. Saddled up his boats and took off. He'll reappear somewhere, with some new scheme. Guys like that always do. But this one's over thanks to you and your friends."

"Are we going home?"

"Not right away," he says. "I've got more research to do. Now that nobody has to be scared of Treasurizers, I think a lot more people are going to want to talk. I'd like your help—and Wave's."

"And Lacey's," you say. "We're a team."

"Well," your uncle agrees, "you're a pretty darn good one."

The End

"How come the water's all brown?"

You have to shout this question to Wave Crawford. You two are standing together at the stern of Lacey Hastings' gleaming white yacht, the *Lace Curtain*.

Ever since you've left Georgetown, the water of the Atlantic Ocean has been surprisingly brown.

"It's from the rivers," he shouts back. "They empty into the ocean near here. If we go out far enough, it turns regular ocean-like."

Looking out from the stern, you admire the amazing flotilla that the *Lace Curtain* is leading.

Spread out behind you, all chugging along, are a dozen or so shrimp trawlers, small commercial fishing boats with little square cabins amidships. The boats are painted white, yellow, bright green, even pink. Each one has its riggings for casting and hauling the shrimp nets, angled outward and upward from the sides of both decks.

Mingled amid the trawlers are several smaller motor launches, open boats that also foray out from Georgetown to drag smaller nets through the water. Shrimping is big business in Guyana—but most of those who go out with their nets are running modest-sized boats, like these.

The *Lace Curtain* is by far the fanciest vessel in this odd flotilla. It's as if a princess, in a white dress, is being trailed by a gaggle of brightly dressed kids out on the water.

It's almost a comical sight. But you can't help wondering: What are you leading these fishermen into? What's going to happen?

Go on to the next page.

After about forty-five minutes steaming away from Georgetown, up ahead you can see the water is starting to turn from river-brown to the blue-green of the ocean.

The *Lace Curtain* slows down.

"We're coming up to it!" Lacey calls down from the flying bridge above you. Lacey is the captain of the *Lace Curtain*, and a skillful sailor. In the main cabin, below the flying bridge, is her first mate, a solemn, slender man named Robert. He and Lacey are in touch by radio phone as he navigates your path to the location on the ocean that Treasurizers so badly wants to keep secret.

"The shrimpers like to cast their nets along this edge, where the shelf drops to deeper water," Wave says. "The fishing's really good along here. That's why it was so bad that they got scared off."

Below you, the color of the water is changing. Lacey calls down, "This is it!"

"The wreck must be down there—where it gets deeper," Wave says, looking down.

You peer into the water. It looks pretty deep to you.

As the boats catch up, Lacey emerges from the bridge with a bullhorn, a portable loudspeaker. When she presses its power button, her voice comes through loud but metallic.

"We are here!" she announces to the shrimp fishermen.

All around you, they lean over their rails to listen.

Turn to the next page.

"You see," Lacey calls through the bullhorn—
"there is nothing! No mist, no ghost ships, no
pirates. You are safe. Go right ahead and fish!"

There is chatter across the water. The shrimp
fishermen seem to agree. One by one across the
scatter of boats, the helmsmen return to their controls. The fishing boats start fanning out across the
water, to do their day's work.

That's when you spot a new boat, approaching
quickly from the west—from the landward side.

This one's a different type of vessel. It's coming
on very fast, knifing through the water.

Go on to the next page.

You alert Lacey. She turns the *Lace Curtain* and powers back the way you've come, to confront the fast-approaching speedboat. Its slender white hull, built for speed, comes to a point that looks as sharp as a knife.

Drawing up alongside it, the *Lace Curtain* slows and so does the speedboat, with a threatening growl of its tall, black, powerful twin outboard engines. Standing there glaring at you through mirrored sunglasses are two muscular-looking men in blue polo shirts.

Then a third man stands up from a bench in the stern. He's got on a white shirt and blue blazer, like a wealthy yachtsman.

"Good morning, Lacey!" the yachtsman calls up to the bridge.

"Hello, Girond," she answers in a less friendly tone.

"Lacey, I'm afraid you've created a situation here," Jeremy Girond says. "We're going to have to deal with it. This is a classified area—we have to keep it secure from prowlers and pirates. I'm sure you understand. Down below us is a very, very valuable site."

Scornfully, Lacey snorts. "Prowlers and pirates? These are fishermen! You can't keep them from earning their living, Girond."

"We can keep them from earning it *here*," he says. "In fact, we are about to do just that."

Turn to the next page.

114

Now Girond smiles. "Admit it, Lacey," he says, "you brought these people out here just to make trouble. For you this is just a game."

"I brought these people here to show them the truth," she snaps. "I don't know if there's really any treasure down there, but I know there's no purple mist!"

"Are you sure?" Girond asks smoothly. "At any rate, do excuse us. We have some work to do."

Girond's boat suddenly cuts its speed. It turns in the water, and seems to stop.

The men on deck are looking back your way.

Now Wave grabs your arm. "Look—down there," he says.

A dark, thick shape seems to be coming up from the blue-green depth, a little distance from the *Lace Curtain*. Is it a giant fish? A deep-water shark?

Whatever it is, it's coming up—and it's coming toward you.

The dark thing that's coming up from below has a smooth, rounded shape. Is it a huge fish?

Go on to the next page.

It's almost to the surface when you two see a thin tube pop up and break the surface, emitting a hissing sound. Purple mist! The mist is thick. And it's coming out fast.

You look up, toward the flying bridge. Lacey is staring off at the Treasurizers boat; she hasn't seen this. Robert's not in the cabin. He must have gone below.

You're startled by a shout from Wave.

"Why, *you're* no jumbie! You not gonna get away with this!"

To your horror, he hops up on the rail. Turning back to you, he shouts: "Go tell Lacey!"

To your amazement and horror, Wave leaps off the boat. Landing in the water atop the just-submerged shape, he grabs the spouting tube.

Now he looks up and shouts, "Throw me down somethin' to stuff into this thing! Some kind of stopper. Do it *quick*!"

Turn to the next page.

116

You look around wildly, then pull up the lid of an equipment locker. Inside is a small rag. Grabbing the towel, you dash back to the rail—but Wave's hidden by the spouting fog. You can't see to throw the rag. Up on the bridge, Lacey's still looking in the opposite direction. She doesn't see any of it.

Go on to the next page.

In a minute, the fog will have swallowed up the whole *Lace Curtain*. Then nobody will be able to see what happens inside the purple cloud. Is that what Girond and his thugs are waiting for? Is that when they'll move in, with their guns?

If you jump in with your improvised plug, you can find Wave and stop up the fog-machine. But if you don't warn Lacey *now*, you could all be put in danger.

If you leap in the water, turn to the next page.

If you warn Lacey, turn to page 126.

118

The water's is so cold it shocks you. You hold tight to the rag, feeling with your feet for the shape of what has to be the Treasurizers minisub.

But there's nothing. You missed it. The fog is covering everything. Treading water while clutching the cloth, you shout, "Wave! *Wave!*"

"Over here!"

You swim through the purple. Gasping for breath, you swallow the acrid, choking chemical fog. Already you're feeling dizzy. You *have* to find your friend.

Then your hand hits something. It's hard metal, just below the surface. Now your knees catch it. You're kneeling on the just-submerged sub. You call: "*Where are you?*"

"Here," he says, close by. "Over here! Can you hear? I'm right..."

Wave's hand reaches through the nasty murk. You grab it and Wave pulls you toward his perch beside the spouting nozzle.

He's coughing, choking in the fog. He sputters, "What've you got?"

You hold the rag up to his eyes. Wave nods, and grabs it.

He stuffs the cloth into the nozzle, but the spouting pressure pushes it out. He says, "Help me!"

Turn to page 120.

Now you're both pushing, fighting the chemical fog, pushing the soaked rag down. Finally, the stream of mist slows, sputters...and stops.

"It won't stay. Too much pressure," Wave says to you. "We've got to hold it!"

But there's a powerful hum beneath you.

And the minisub starts to move.

As you both clutch the stem and hold onto your ragged plug, the sub moves away from the curtain of purple fog.

"Swim for the boat," Wave gasps.

"*What?*"

"You got to swim for the boat! Lacey can't see us. They goin' to try to drown us. You got to swim *now.*"

Clutching the spout, Wave looks desperately at you. The sub is moving away from the fog. You have to decide.

If you swim for help, go on to the next page.

If you stay with Wave, turn to page 124.

"Okay, I'll go for it," you shout to Wave. "Hold on! Don't let go!"

"Why'd I wanna do anything else?" he shouts back. "Swim *fast*."

You take a deep breath, then push off.

You're swimming in choppy water toward a shifting purple curtain of fog.

You can't see the *Lace Curtain*—but the ocean breezes are ruffling and moving the purple fog. It's starting to break up. If you can just keep going...

There's the powerful blast of a ship's horn. You look up to see the bow of a white boat slicing through the purple. But which white boat is it— Lacey's or Girond's?

You stop swimming and tread water, bobbing up and down for the second that it takes...for the bow to be followed by the midsection and tall flying bridge of the *Lace Curtain*.

Kicking hard to lift yourself up in the water, you wave your arms wildly. The horn sounds again— and up on the bridge you see Lacey, waving her arms.

You spin in the water, looking back. Wave is hanging on, you see his arm waving at you.

Then he disappears beneath the water.

Turn to the next page.

When the *Lace Curtain* reaches you, Robert is leaning over the rail. He throws down a lifejacket.

"Put that on and climb up—there's a ladder on the stern," he yells down.

You want to yell back that you'll be fine, for now—he should go find Wave. You're sure the sub dove under water. That means your friend is out there, with nothing to hold onto.

And, you realize, only you know where he'd be.

But *do* you know? Suddenly panicked, you whirl around in the water.

Out on the ocean, there are no landmarks. You look in the direction where you're sure Wave was.

Above the horizon, a single fluffy cloud hovers in the sky. That's your marker—*if* you can get on the boat quickly.

Leaving the lifejacket behind, you swim fast for the stern of the yacht. You wonder, what are Girond and his thugs doing?

They were waiting for the fog to hide the yacht—that seems clear. But...maybe that didn't happen. Because you and Wave plugged the spout.

Seizing the ladder at the stern of the *Lace Curtain,* you scramble up. Robert reaches down and hauls you in.

You spin around. The cloud...where is it?

"There," you point. "We have to go that way!"

And at that moment, looking that way you see a pair of arms. Just above the water, Wave is waving.

We're going to be okay, you think. *We're going to be okay.*

The End

You realize Wave is too tired to swim fast. Getting behind him, you wrap one arm around his chest and kick and kick.

Then you see the *Lace Curtain* come through the fog—and you wave wildly with your free arm.

Minutes later, Wave is still shivering, sitting up on deck with you wrapped in towels from neck to toe. The purple mist machine is long gone. Robert has taken the wheel so Lacey can join her team.

"Jeremy Girond is finished," she says. "I mean it. He's *done*."

You ask, "How? What are you going to do?"

Lacey's eyes blaze with righteous anger.

"First of all," she says, "his scary purple mist was just a chemical fog—and everyone saw that.

"As soon as we dock," she says, "I'm going to the Princess Hotel to have a nice little chat with each one of his investors. Some are in the hotel, and the others I can reach by phone. Don't worry—I know every one of them. I'll shoot so many holes in his fake-fog, fake-pirate, fake-treasure scheme, there'll be nothing left *but* holes.

"Now," she says. "Let's talk about our team."

Go on to the next page.

"First of all," Lacey says to you, "you and your uncle are going to come stay with me—on the *Lace Curtain.*"

"Um...it's totally nice here," you say. "But I really like being with the Crawfords."

"Well, sure. That's fine," she says. "But meanwhile, your uncle is going to write the best book he's ever done. I'm going to pay his expenses— and we'll keep on being his investigators. We are going to make sure Jeremy Girond, the international scam artist, is exposed to the whole world. Whatever we need to do, I promise you: we will do it."

The End

After that terrible day, the myth of the purple mist only grows—and so does the mystery.

Churning back to Georgetown, the shrimp fishermen scramble onto the waterfront with a shocking tale. They tell friends and family that the rich American lady in her white yacht led them out to the place of the strange mist.

Everything was fine, she assured them. They could go about their business here, just like before.

But when they did, the shrimpers say, something terrible happened. The purple mist was real!

Those who were still close enough to the American yacht, to see, said the purple fog rose as if by magic from the water. It swallowed the white boat completely. Nothing else could be seen: just a huge purple cloud, spreading across the ocean and rising to the sky.

Then the fishermen swore they heard gunfire. It was as if the jumbie ship, the ghost vessel of pirates, was real—and was attacking the yacht.

Go on to the next page.

The shrimpers were too terrified to approach the cloud. But when it finally broke up and drifted away, there was nothing there. No sign of a yacht. It was as if it had been lifted up into the spirit world—into the realm of the jumbies.

All that was left on the water, they reported, was an oily purple sheen. That could have been an oil slick, left by a sunken yacht. But the shrimpers are sure it was, instead, the last remnant of the purple pirate mist.

Before long, everybody on the waterfront has heard this terrifying tale.

And by now, everyone believes it.

Turn to the next page.

Or perhaps the American boat had sunk to the bottom of the ocean. That also, the shrimpers had to admit, was possible.

They were scared to go close to the site; but from a distance, there looked to be, perhaps, a purplish sheen on the water. It could have been the telltale oil slick of a sunken ship, just like the bauxite freighters left, back in the war when they were torpedoed by the German subs.

It could have been an oil slick. Or it could have been a last vestige of the jumbie cloud.

Either way the American lady and her fancy boat, and the kids, had disappeared. After that, every shrimper in Georgetown harbor believed in the jumbie cloud. No boat ever went near that section of the offshore waters again.

That left Jeremy Girond and his crew free to mount their treasure-salvage operation on that same spot. Which they did. After your disappearance, your uncle returns home, so traumatized that he never writes another book. But Girond, who becomes the host of the reality TV show *Ocean of Mysteries*, becomes world-famous. And quite rich.

He never actually finds any treasure. But he always seems to find amazing mysteries to explore. Such as a fabled purple mist, and the local fishermen's belief that inside it hides the ghost of a pirate ship—one that remains, somehow, just as murderous as it was in the old times.

The End

This really was risky, your uncle had explained to the cameras. If the ROV were to get trapped inside the ship and couldn't get out, the show would be over.

Somehow, you doubted that would happen. Jeremy Girond is set to make millions from the show, there's no way he'd let it all end.

And it *is* exciting watching the submersible swim into the murky ship's interior. The ROV's high-intensity lamps light up a weird, shadowy world. You've seen strange shapes and odd encrustations.

Today, as the ROV carefully moves deeper in, the cameras locate something. It was squarish, a pile of objects.

The objects were all the same, silvery bars stacked on top of each other.

"Oh my god," says one of the ROV operators, his hands frozen on the controls.

"*Ingots*," another technician whispers.

As the show's host, your uncle steps in to explain.

"Ingots are the form that valuable metal is first made into, after it is processed and refined from its original ore," he tells the video cameras. "And that's...that's a *lot* of ingots."

It's true. As the ROV drew closer, the stack of silvery bars appear larger. Taller.

"Hundreds of them," someone murmurs.

"Are they silver?" someone else asks

"They sure look like it," said the ROV operator. "Let's see if we can grab one. Bring it up."

And that's what they do.

Go on to the next page.

Standing on deck a little while later, you're watching the odd expression on Jeremy Girond's face. He's very surprised. He looks confused. You feel even more sure that Girond never *really* thought they'd find treasure inside this sunken ship. He just wanted to create a show about *searching* for treasure.

Now the ROV breaks the surface, with a sound like dripping suction. A crane on deck swoops down, latches onto the submersible and picks it up, like a giant insect arm lifting a square-backed, mechanical spider.

The ingot in the spider's claw is surprisingly small. It's also surprisingly clean looking, even after decades at the bottom of the ocean. No corrosion. Its color is a dull silver.

Crew members pull on rubber gloves. Very carefully, they open their hands below the robot claw. At Girond's signal, the claw is opened.

The ingot drops into a crew member's palm. And when it does...he sighs.

"It's light," he says, hefting the ingot to feel its weight. "Very light."

You turn to your uncle. You ask, "What does that mean?"

Turn to the next page.

132

"May I?" he asks. The crew member nods, and places the ingot in your uncle's hand. He also feels its weight.

And now your uncle sighs.

"During World War II," he says to the camera, "British Guiana was the world's largest producer of a metal that was very, very precious indeed."

So it *is* a precious metal! But then, why is your uncle's tone so serious?

"This metal was vital," your uncle goes on, "for building the aircraft that would go on to win the war. It bent into different shapes easily and almost incredibly: it simply wouldn't rust. It was very strong and it was..." he hefts the ingot onto his palm, "amazingly light."

Go on to the next page.

"To save on shipping costs, Britain built a big processing plant in Guiana, to extract this metal from an ore that is mined here, and shape it into ingots like these. Those were transported to aircraft and warship factories, in Great Britain and the U.S.

"This ingot was hugely valuable, to the war effort then," your uncle says. "Today...well, aluminum is still worth *something*, as an industrial metal. But if that pile of ingots down there had been actual silver—instead of just *looking* like silver—well..."

Girond nods.

"We'd have all been rich beyond our wildest dreams," he says.

"And it's really the dream that treasure hunting is all about," your uncle says. "Don't you agree?"

For the video cameras, Jeremy Girond smiles.

"Sure," he agrees, "It's all about the search. And maybe tomorrow we'll find the *real* treasure," he tells the cameras.

The cameras switch off. And Girond's smile disappears.

"For a second there," he mutters, "I almost believed it *was* real."

Your uncle catches your eye, and shrugs. He says, "Welcome to..."

"I know," you interrupt. "Welcome to the crazy world of treasure hunters."

The End

About the Illustrators

Gabhor Utomo was born in Indonesia. He moved to California to pursue his passion in art. He received his degree from Academy of Art University in San Francisco in spring 2003. Since his graduation he has worked as a freelance illustrator and has illustrated a number of children's books. Gabhor lives with his wife Dina and his twin girls in the San Francisco Bay Area.

Vladimir Semionov was born in August 1964 in the Republic of Moldavia, of the former USSR. He is a graduate of the Fine Arts Collegium in Kishinev, Moldavia, as well as the Fine Arts Academy of Romania, where he majored in graphics and painting, respectively. He has had exhibitions all over the world, in places like Japan and Switzerland, and is currently Art Director of the SEM&BL Animacompany animation studio in Bucharest.

About the Author

Doug Wilhelm is the author of eight previous Choose Your Own Adventure titles, as well as *The Revealers*, a novel about bullying that has been read and discussed in hundreds of middle schools. *True Shoes*, a sequel to *The Revealers*, is being published in December 2011. Doug's other young-adult novels include *Falling* and *Raising the Shades*. He lives in Weybridge, Vermont.

For games, activities, and other fun stuff, or to write to Doug, visit us online at CYOA.com